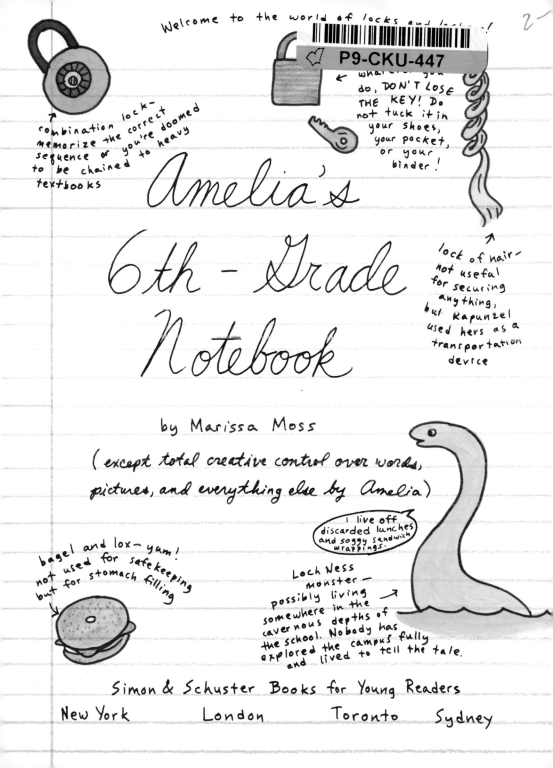

Welcome to the world of locks and locks!

combination lock— memorize the correct sequence or you're doomed to be chained to heavy textbooks

whatever you do, DON'T LOSE THE KEY! Do not tuck it in your shoes, your pocket, or your binder!

lock of hair— not useful for securing anything, but Rapunzel used hers as a transportation device

Amelia's 6th - Grade Notebook

by Marissa Moss

(except total creative control over words, pictures, and everything else by Amelia)

I live off discarded lunches and soggy sandwich wrappings.

bagel and lox— yum! not used for safekeeping but for stomach filling

Loch Ness monster— possibly living somewhere in the cavernous depths of the school. Nobody has explored the campus fully and lived to tell the tale.

Simon & Schuster Books for Young Readers

New York   London   Toronto   Sydney

SIMON & SCHUSTER BOOKS FOR YOUNG READERS
An imprint of Simon & Schuster Publishing Division
1230 Avenue of the Americas, New York, New York 10020

Imprint—
NOT footprint!

No
triangles,
circles,
or squares!

SIMON & SCHUSTER BOOKS FOR YOUNG READERS
IS A TRADEMARK OF SIMON & SCHUSTER, INC.
Amelia® and the notebook design are
registered trademarks of Marissa Moss.

Book design by Amelia
(with help from Lucy Ruth Cummins)

Thanks,
Lucy! →

The text for this book is hand-lettered.

↑ And is my hand tired!

Manufactured in the USA
4 6 8 10 9 7 5 3

Library of Congress Cataloging-in-Publication Data

Moss, Marissa.
Amelia's sixth-grade notebook/Marissa Moss.— 1st ed.
p. cm.
Summary: Problems arise for Amelia
when she starts sixth grade at the same middle
school where her older sister, Cleo, is an eighth
grader, and she gets the school's meanest teacher for
three of her classes.
ISBN 0-689-87040-X
[1. Schools—Fiction. 2. Sisters—Fiction. 3. Teachers—Fiction.
4. Diaries—Fiction] I. Title.
PZ7.M8535 An 2005
[Fic] —dc22
2004045309

Amelia's 6th-Grade Notebook

At last!

It seems like there should be a BIG change in me, but I still look the same. →

← I mean, some 6th-grade girls already look like teenagers with bras and makeup. I still look closer to 6 than 16.

Here I am, officially a 6th grader, even though school doesn't begin until tomorrow. The good thing about starting middle school is I'll get a locker and change classes every period like in high school. And there will be a real lab for science and real experiments we can do, not just baking-soda volcanos.

this →

cool, mysterious chemicals — VERY DANGEROUS! Do not get on your skin and DEFINITELY DO NOT SWALLOW!

not this ↘

ordinary stuff you can find in your kitchen — you could even eat it if you wanted to (not that it would taste good, but it wouldn't kill you)

There's only one bad thing, but it's a BIG bad thing.

CLEO!

I won't be in the same class as my obnoxious older sister since she's in 8th grade, but I'll be in the same school. Our universes will collide! We might even see each other during lunch. (Now that's a stomach-turning proposition. I'll have to listen to Cleo chomping at school as well as at home. Yuucch!)

Cleo's not giving me a friendly welcome either. She <u>could</u> help me out with hints and tips (like telling me which bathrooms are waaay too gross to use and which are bearable). Instead, she's warning me to stay away from her. I guess she doesn't want to share her school with me any more than I want to share it with her. But it's not like we have a choice.

beady eyes glaring →

← jelly roll nose flaring

I'm NOT walking to school with you, you know, NO WAY!

And if you even try to talk to me, I'll pretend I don't know you.

As if <u>I</u> want anyone to know she's my sister!

No wonder I don't know how to look like I belong in middle school. Look at the model I have to follow!

I don't find out my classes until the first day of school, but I hope that I have the same schedule as Carly — and that my classes are as far away from Cleo's as possible.

Luckily the school tries to keep the 8th graders away from the 6th graders, like the older kids are wild beasts dangerous to young children. They do look like another species, like grown-ups already. (But don't tell them that!)

No way!   Way!   Way way!

6TH GRADERS ONLY SECTION — ANYONE ELSE

KEEP OUT!

snotty clique of 8th-grade girls — they even speak their own language. NOTHING is scarier!

Anyway, the school is SO big and SO confusing, it would be a miracle if I see <u>anyone</u> I recognize. I need more than a map for finding my classes — I need a Global Positioning System!

← Principal's office — here's a place you don't want to find!

Staircase X — leads to the 2nd floor, but only to rooms 2003 to 2027. For the other 2nd floor rooms, there's a completely different staircase, but I still haven't figured out where it is.

Gym — another place that's easy to find but harder to escape — the stink of thousands of damp armpits throughout history clogs your nose as soon as you enter.

If you go down the wrong corridor, you may never be heard from again!

Bathrooms — WARNING! Entering may be hazardous to your health — the stench could kill you!

← piles of garbage = 26

← rolls of toilet paper = 0

The heart of the maze is the mystical hall of lockers. You can find it once to put your stuff in, but never again!

Staircase Q — leads to 2nd floor on Tuesdays and Thursdays, but on Mondays and Wednesdays leads to janitor's closet, and on Fridays, who knows?

At least you can always find the cafeteria — just follow the smell of boiled rubber and burnt underwear.

Staircase Z — leads to an alternate universe

Where to sit at lunch is another puzzle. There's the cool table, the nerd table, and the outcast table, but what I need is to eat lunch without being ranked, rated, or labeled, so where can I sit? Do I have to eat in the bathroom?

The aliens await you! All strange species welcome here!

I finally found my classes, but now I wish I hadn't. The only bad thing about middle school isn't breathing the same air as Cleo — there's something even WORSE — much. MUCH WORSE — and his name is Mr. Lambaste.

Single eyebrow makes him look even grumpier.

Everything about him is straight, tight, and thin.

narrow eyes that get narrower when he calls on you

mouth with no lips, like an angry slash in his face

Don't be fooled by the bow tie. You think you would have to have a sense of humor to wear one of these, but Mr. Lambaste proves that's not true.

I thought everyone had eyelashes, but not Mr. Lambaste. I think it's because his eyes are so icy cold, lashes can't grow on the lids.

voice like frozen metal

Now I find out he's the meanest, most notorious teacher in the whole school — everyone hates him! When I tell kids he's my teacher, they look at me like I just told them I have a horrible disease.

Luckily in middle school there's a different teacher for every subject, so at least I don't have Mr. Lambaste all day, BUT I have him more than any other teacher — for English, social studies, and homeroom. The worst should NEVER be the most. That makes the worst even worse, like worst to the tenth power or mega-worst. And to make that more unbearable, the classes I have with Mr. Lambaste are exactly the same classes I don't have with Carly, my best friend.

Friends are like air bags — you need them as a buffer to protect you from injury — like when you're eating lunch alone, facing bullies, or dealing with mean teachers.

Carly and I compared schedules first thing.
↓

One thing I like about Carly is that she's a natural 6th grader — not like me. ↓

Maybe some of her coolness will rub off on me. I'm definitely not cool, but I'm not sure what to change. Maybe everything!

she's tall → and pretty and knows how to dress. She even wears a bra!

The schedule is more complicated than the train schedule Dad brought back from his trip to Russia — you know, Track 62 at 10:41 a.m. train to Siberia except on alternate Wednesdays when it goes to Plotsk and Sundays when it goes to Yamutz ... unless traveling in a month with the letter "R," when the opposite is the case. That's my class schedule — English is 1st period on A weeks but only on Mondays and Wednesdays, except when there's a full moon and then it's last. On B weeks, of course, English is 3rd period, unless "i" before "e" except after "c" or when sounded like "ay" as in "neighbor" or "weigh."

Now I not only have to worry about _where_ my classes are — I have to worry about _when_ they are. It's more confusing than memorizing the quadratic equation! →

As if I didn't have enough to deal with just finding my way in the vast new world of middle school, now I have to navigate the minefield of an explosive teacher. It's all too much — I'm ready for summer vacation and school just started!

PERILS OF MIDDLE SCHOOL

intimidating 8th graders

intimidating 7th graders

intimidating 6th graders

Excuse me!

I can't sit next to you at lunch until I know what kind of car your dad drives.

That's okay. I can't sit next to you until I know how often you change underwear.

You're breathing my air!

Um, do you mind? You're blocking out the sun.

oh-so-cool kid — could I possibly be like this in just one year?

intimidating teachers

Just to start us off on the right foot, here are the rules: no talking out of turn and no leaning back in your chairs.

No laughing, yawning, spitting, or snorting. No flatulence or flatulence jokes. No tardies, no unexplained absences, and no excuses.

Do we understand each other now?

I've always had nice teachers. I mean, I thought all teachers liked kids or they wouldn't __be__ teachers. Not Mr. Lambaste. He __hates__ kids. And most of all, he hates me. I could tell right away.

I wanted to rinse out my mouth after class to get out the bad taste of Mr. Lambaste. Except I've already learned that none of the drinking fountains here is decent. And I was afraid my other teachers would be as bad as him, but they're okay.

Mrs. Church, my math teacher. Nothing can make math good, but at least she's not mean. And she tries to make math fun — she just doesn't know that's an impossible task.

helmet hair — her head turns, but the hair doesn't move with it, it's so stiff!

> Now, class, fractions are our friends!

But not the kind of friends you invite to a sleepover, not the kind of friends you want to spend any time with.

Bright orange lipstick (which matches her bright orange nail polish) makes it distracting to watch her speak because her mouth looks like one of those gross orange peanut candies — the kind only old people eat that have nothing to do with tasting good. Instead of paying attention to what she says, I can't help thinking about whoever invented those candy peanuts in the first place and why, with all the new candy that's been invented since then, are those peanuts still being made? It's one of those unsolved mysteries of mankind.

WATER HAZARDS
↓

↑ gum-encrusted

↑ mud-filled

broken — no water at all

broken — too much water that shoots up your nose

↑ clogged with mysterious green slime — I don't want to know what it could be!

Ms. Reilly, my science teacher — she's from Ireland, and I love listening to her accent. No matter what she says, it sounds great. →

We have a lot to cover this year, so I expect you to work hard. But it will be a fun kind of hard because we're starting off the year with biology, so we'll have the chance to do some dissections.

← music to my ears — not the words, but the tone of them

Wait a minute! Did she say "dissections"?! As in cutting something open and looking at its insides? I wonder if I can plead being a conscientious objector and do some kind of community service like erasing blackboards instead. (Or I could stock the bathrooms with soap and toilet paper — that'd be a _real_ service.)

Suddenly the jars of strange things floating in formaldehyde looked really creepy. Are those the kinds of things we'll be cutting open?

mysterious chemicals in mysterious colors ↘

All the gleaming sinks and test tubes looked really cool, like in a real scientific lab, but maybe science isn't for me after all. I wish we could skip biology and go right to chemistry.

For foreign language I'm taking French because that's what Carly's taking, even though we didn't end up in the same class. Maybe next semester...

Monsieur Le Poivre (that's Mr. Pepper in English!) — just to show you how tricky French is, take the word for mister, "monsieur." It looks like you would pronounce it "mon-see-ur" or "mon-soo-er," but you're supposed to say "mah-syur." Who would ever guess that?

Allez, les enfants, au travail!

↑ translation: "Come on, kids, get to work!"

The best thing about Monsieur (however you say it!) Le Poivre is that he has a HUGE collection of comic books. He calls them "bandes dessinées," and he says in France they're considered an art form. That means the comics I do are works of art! I knew it!

our textbooks— YAY!! ←   →

my first bande dessinée
↓

Ah, choux!

Bless you! You must have a cold.

A cold?

I'm not sneezing. I didn't say ah-choo.

...but ah, choux— that's French for cabbage— delicious!

Then there's the dreaded PE class with the dreaded PE teacher.

Mr. Klein takes himself way too seriously — it's just PE — not astrophysics!

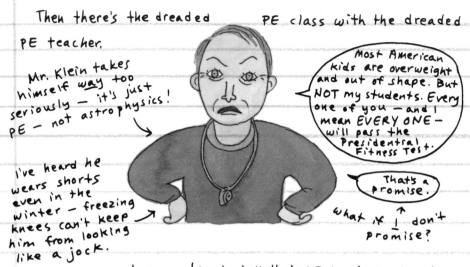

Most American kids are overweight and out of shape. But NOT my students. Every one of you — and I mean EVERY ONE — will pass the Presidential Fitness Test.

That's a promise.

What if I don't promise?

I've heard he wears shorts even in the winter — freezing knees can't keep him from looking like a jock.

I can already tell that PE is NOT going to be a good class for me. Not just because of Mr. Klein, either. We have to wear the UGLIEST uniform possible, and the smallest size is WAY too big for me. I'm afraid if I run, the shorts will fall off.

Did you ever wonder who designs PE uniforms anyway? I mean, could someone have <u>intentionally</u> chosen a nerdier style? I don't think so! It's as if some evil gym teacher spent days thinking of the most embarrassing possible outfit.

maniacal uniform designer

Heee, heee, heee! Let's have the shirt be as lumpy as it can get.

It will look like a potato sack on skinny kids, like a tube of toothpaste on fat kids, and like a dishrag on kids in between.

Let's see 'em TRY to run in this!

My last class is art. I thought it would be my favorite. Now I'm not so sure. I mean, I still like art, I'm just not sure about the teacher.

Ms. Oates — except she wants us to call her "Star." That's her inner artist name. I wonder if she has an inner baker or reader or sleeper.

You can't let your creative spirit flow until you have the tools to express it.

This class will give you those tools so you can spread your wings and soar.

She's an artist herself (I mean, not just an art teacher), which is good, but she has some weird weird weird weird ideas that aren't so good.

No matter what grade I'm in, spelling this word is always a problem!

I thought by tools she meant pens and pencils or paints and brushes. But she's not letting us use any cool art supplies yet. Today we used plain old pencils, the kind you use for homework, not even those special sketch pencils with soft, dark lead that make you feel like a real artist just by holding them. And all we did was draw on regular old plain paper. Big deal! I do that every day anyway — I don't need a class for that!

Except Ms. Oates — I mean, Star — made us use the left hand if we're right-handed or the right hand if we're left-handed. It was like she was showing us how NOT to draw.

My left hand is a <u>terrible</u> artist. It doesn't even know how to hold a pencil. Star said this would help us <u>see</u> better. All I saw was a clumsy drawing.

With my left hand I draw the same way I did when I was two... this is an improvement?

At least Leah's in my art class. She's a good artist, but even she couldn't make a decent picture with her right hand (because <u>she's</u> left-handed).

I feel like I'm drawing with a potato!

Is this supposed to make <u>her</u> art look good?

I'm not sure.

But I feel like I'm back in preschool— NOT middle school.

If this seems horrible, I just need to remember it's better than drawing with my toes — barely!

I know some of the kids in some of my classes, and at least I have Carly and Leah in 3 classes. But that still leaves 4 classes without a possible ally. I need to make some new friends fast— especially in Mr. Lambaste's classes. I can't face him alone. It's tricky not being in the same class all day. I was excited about changing teachers, but I forgot that also meant a new group of students each time too. So now I not only have to get used to all my different teachers, I have to get used to a bunch of different kids. IT'S EXHAUSTING!! I've never wanted to be homeschooled before, but it's beginning to sound good. Except for Cleo 24/7 — UGH! I guess this is better.

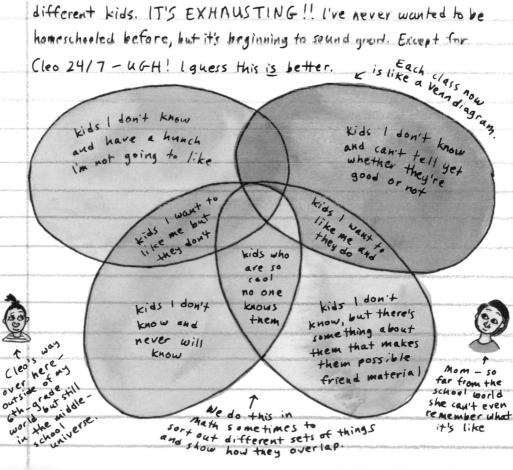

← Each class now is like a Venn diagram.

kids I don't know and have a hunch I'm not going to like

Kids I don't know and can't tell yet whether they're good or not

kids I want to like me but they don't

kids I want to like me and they do

kids who are so cool no one knows them

kids I don't know and never will know

kids I don't know, but there's something about them that makes them possible friend material

↑ Cleo's way over here— outside of my 6th-grade world but still in the middle-school universe.

↑ We do this in math sometimes to sort out different sets of things and show how they overlap.

↑ Mom — so far from the school world she can't even remember what it's like

Besides dealing with the human aspects of middle school (I mean teachers and students), there are the non-human problems. Difficulty number 1 is: The Locker. You don't just put books into the locker and forget about them — you put them in, you take them out, you forget things in the locker, you squash things there (mostly my lunch). You're always running back and forth to that stupid locker. And it doesn't mean you don't have to carry as much stuff like I thought. I have so many heavy textbooks now my backpack weighs a ton. I thought it would be cool to have a locker and NOT lug around books, but the locker is only good to hold books while you're in class. You still have to take them all home for homework.

Don't let this happen to you!

↓

I can't get up!

Help! I'm being crushed by a two-ton backpack!

↑
Instead of feeling like a cool big kid, I feel like a bug being squashed.

↑
If you lose your balance and fall over, you're done for! You'll never be able to get up without a crane!

And having a locker means remembering your locker combination — as if you don't already have enough junk to memorize in school. The first day I was okay with the combination since I wrote it down in my notebook. The problem was, I forgot which <u>locker</u> was mine!

seen one locker... →  ←...seen 'em all!

Of course, even on the first day there was homework.

Middle school is <u>serious</u>, not like elementary school.

no more Valentine's Day parties with pink cupcakes and punch
↓

no more art projects gluing beans and noodles on construction paper
↓

no more playing tetherball
↓

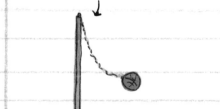

no more decorating the classroom for holidays
↓

no more smell of glue and paste at your desk
↓

no more using sequins for art and sneaking some in your pockets to take home
↓

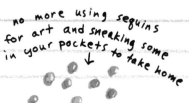

no more being read to by the teacher
↓

I'm going to miss all that stuff. So far all middle school has replaced it with is more homework, lockers, and mean teachers like Mr. Lambaste. Not a good trade, if you ask me. And that doesn't even include worrying about where to sit for lunch, wearing ugly PE uniforms, and trying to figure out how to be cool and how NOT to be a nerd. Learning stuff is the LEAST of the work I have to deal with now! Each day is like a tricky maze — I have to avoid traps and come out the other side alive!

All kinds of nasty surprises lurk around every corner — you never know what you'll encounter. →

EEEEK!

HELP!

FREE AT LAST!

At dinner Mom asked how school was. I didn't want to complain, but I couldn't help mentioning Mr. Lambaste and how mean he is. Cleo laughed so hard, milk shot out of her nose.

Cleo is so charming — NOT!
↓

HA HA HA HA

← duck and cover — quick!

I didn't see what was so funny.

Cleo finally calmed down enough to tell me — after she'd sprayed my dinner with milk snot. GROSS!

daintily dabbing her nose →

You have terrible luck. Mr. Lambaste is the meanest teacher in the whole school. I had him in 6th grade too, and he absolutely hated me. You're in for it now.

"What do you mean, I'm in for it?" I asked.

Cleo looked at Mom. I could see there was something she didn't want Mom to know.

"I'll tell you later," she whispered.

Whatever it was, I could tell it was BAD. Suddenly I wasn't hungry anymore (as if milk blasting from nostrils isn't enough to make you lose your appetite).

↑ Mom could tell too that Cleo was hiding something. It's hard to fool her. When I was little, I believed Mom when she said she had eyes in the back of her head.

I was doing my homework when Cleo came into my room.

So you want to know about me and Mr. Lambaste?

I have a feeling I really don't.

Come on — you want to know why he hates me, don't you?

I was tempted to say, "Because you're Cleo," but I didn't.

"I played a trick on him," Cleo said. She looked happy about it. "You know how he always has a cup of coffee on his desk — well, you don't know yet, but believe me, he does. Anyway, I snuck some salt into it when he wasn't looking. A LOT of salt."

I stared at her. I couldn't believe Cleo could really be that obnoxious. And I live with her. We're even (GAGGG!) related. I know how nasty she can be. But that's to me or Mom, not to a TEACHER! That's a whole new level of Cleoness (or is it Cleo-ocity?).

"Did he drink it?" I asked. Part of me didn't want to know the answer, but part of me really needed to know the worst.

innocent cup of coffee or toxic sludge? ⟶

looks like coffee, smells like coffee, tastes like ? ←

Cleo actually looked proud of herself. She grinned like she'd just won a gold medal in Teacher Trickery.

"He took a BIG swallow! It was so awful, he spit it out — all over this poor kid in the front row!"

coffee attack on innocent bystander (or if you're at a desk, are you a bysitter?)

HELP!

CALL 911!

SAVE ME!

unfortunate victim had to smell like a diner all day.

coffee-stained textbook — who pays for the damages?

Cleo laughed, remembering it. "You should have seen his face. It was HILARIOUS!"

"And?" I asked. It didn't sound so funny to me. And I felt sorry for the kid who got spattered with coffee.

"And what?" Cleo asked.

"And did he find out it was you who put in the salt?"

Cleo suddenly got very serious. "I don't know how he figured it out. He just <u>knew</u>. I had detention for a month. But I never confessed! He may have suspected me and punished me for it, but he never could prove anything."

"Too bad for you," I said. "But what does any of this have to do with me?"

"You're my sister."

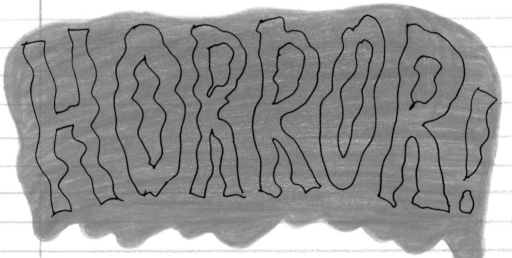

Does that mean that Mr. Lambaste looks at me and sees Cleo? Is he angry at me because he's still mad at Cleo — two years later? But I'm NOTHING like her. That's totally NOT fair! Why should <u>I</u> be punished for something <u>she</u> did?

what I am ↓

what Mr. Lambaste sees ↙

↑
sweet, innocent girl — always a good student, not the kind who plays tricks on teachers, has never had detention in her life

↑
evil, rude, nose-picking girl — exactly the type to snort milk out her nose and pour salt into an unsuspecting teacher's cup of coffee

↑
Maybe I should just wear a paper bag?

Maybe I should change my last name. Or maybe I should tell Mr. Lambaste that even though Cleo and I have the same last name, it's just a coincidence — we're NOT related.

It's bad enough that I have to worry what students think of me, now I have to worry about what kind of reputation teachers think I have. I wish I could change my face and be someone completely new — someone who kids think is cool, someone who teachers want in their class, someone like Carly. Why am I stuck being me? Worst of all, why am I stuck being Cleo's sister?

My hair is too short to do anything with — I tried to make a different style. Maybe I should just dye it purple? ↙

Or I could make my hair even shorter, but then everyone would think I'm a boy. ↓ The only thing worse than being Cleo's sister would be being her brother!

I couldn't decide what to do, so I wrote to Nadia. Even though she lives far away, she's still one of my best friends. It always helps me to explain my problems to her. ↓

Dear Nadia,
I wish we were in the same middle school and you didn't live so far away. If I could move back there, I would!
I mean, school here is mostly good, but there's one BIG problem. I have a very mean teacher named Mr. Lambaste, and the reason he's so mean is that Cleo played a trick on him when she was in 6th grade. Even though I didn't do anything, he hates me. He looks at me and he sees Cleo. UGH! I have a feeling this will be a very looooong year.
Yours till the paper cuts, Amelia

23¢
FLYING
BABIES

Nadia Kurz
61 South St.
Barton, CA
91010

I didn't explain the details of the problem. It all seems so complicated. But Nadia will know what I mean. She understands Cleo's reputation and how awful it would be to live under its shadow. It's like being marked by an ugly scar or a terrible stink cloud wherever you go.

Today was even worse than yesterday. Cleo's right — Mr. Lambaste really has it in for me. He gave back the pop quiz from yesterday, and he marked me down for using the word "mad" instead of "angry."

I shouldn't have complained, but it was so unfair I couldn't help myself.

Um, Mr. Lambaste, I think there's a mistake on my grade. See, you marked off for "mad," but that's the same as "angry."

Is it? Is it really? Mad can mean crazy.

Angry doesn't. The mistake was yours, not mine!

I was so nervous my hands were shaking.

cup of coffee — a bad reminder

His voice was cold and hissy, like sharp stabbing needles.

Great, I thought, now I've really made him angry — or should I say mad, since he's both crazy and irritated? All the kids say he's like that — he has his favorites, and if you're not one of them, watch out! And he has the kids he likes to pick on. If you're one of those — and I am — then you really have to watch out.

When I saw Carly at lunch, she could tell right away something was wrong.

Amelia, you're shaking! What happened?

I feel like Mr. Lambaste beat me up with his icy words.

He's so mean!

I was so upset, I didn't even notice I was sitting at the wrong table, the preppie table. How unlucky can you get! Good thing Carly rescued me.

The whole school is a maze, but navigating the cafeteria is tricky by itself. I never realized how much it mattered <u>where</u> you sat and <u>who</u> you ate lunch with. In my old school I just cared about what was <u>in</u> my lunch. Not anymore. Food is the least important part of lunch now. There are so many separate groups of kids, I'm not sure where I belong. But I know where I <u>don't</u> belong — and the preppie table is definitely not for me! Carly nudged me away, and we sat on a bench by ourselves. If you have one good friend to be with, the rest doesn't matter.

The athletes' table (beware of loud burps and spattering ketchup!)
Pass the ketchup - I need more!
Did you see those A's?
And how about the Niners? What a great game!
The school spirit table
Rah!
Rah!
Rah!
Hey, why aren't you wearing the school colors? What's wrong with you?
The artists' table
I was just trying to be creative, but the teacher wouldn't accept my collage as a book report.
How fascist!
I thought I might belong at this table, but my artistic vocabulary isn't strong enough for the way they talk. I don't know what neo-expressionist means. And I don't care, either.
The theater table
Iced tea, iced tea! My kingdom for iced tea!
Don't be so melo-dramatic.
Can you mime that?
This looks like a fun table, but I can't act. The biggest part I've ever had was the corn in the Thanksgiving play.

I'm lucky I have Carly to sit with. I told her what happened with Mr. Lambaste. I wish I was in _her_ English and social studies class. She has Ms. Amina – a normal teacher, not a bully.

"Just ignore him," Carly said. But some things you just can't ignore. A teacher who hates you is one of them.

Ignorable ↓   Not Ignorable ↓

If I stick my nose in this bag of popcorn, I'll be fine.

Oh, baby, oh, marsh-mallow pie-ie-ie-ie...

...oh, baby, oh, spit in my eye, eye, eye...

the smell of a fart

Cleo singing

BZZZZZZ

WEEEE EEEEE

a fly buzzing around

I vant to suck your blood!

the whine of a mosquito

Believe me, this will hurt YOU way more than me!

the whistle of a teakettle

Hmmm— nice tone. sounds like an A flat.

the warning of a skunk lifting its tail

It's not just Mr. Lambaste that makes school hard (though he's the worst). There's a lot to get used to in middle school. I have to remember how to find my classes, when to find them, my locker combination (and where my locker is), my homework, AND where I'm supposed to sit in the cafeteria.

Homework is a whole separate problem. Suddenly there's a TON of it. Instead of having one teacher assign maybe an hour a night, I have five different teachers, each with their hour of homework to do. That's almost as many hours of homework as there are in a school day!

I didn't sleep at all last night.

But I got my homework done.

How long can someone last like this, not sleeping?

I mean, this is middle school, NOT night school! Aren't students supposed to get a good night's sleep?

At least with different teachers I don't have Mr. Lambaste all day — THAT would be a real nightmare!

Still, it would be better if we could start middle school step-by-step instead of everything all at once, like gradually sticking your toes into the water instead of being shoved in all at once, and you're not sure if you'll swim or sink to the bottom or get water up your nose.

But there are good things too. I **LOVE** science! We get to use real scientific equipment (and no dissections yet)!

microscope ↓

Bunsen burner—
yum! I love the smell of smoldering science ↓

test tube ↓

glass beaker with mysterious chemical ↓

? ↘ science!

↖ Mix them all together and you get science!

I would love to make a real secret potion. I know just what I would make.

Anti-
Mr. Hyde
Potion →

Instead of drinking a mixture and turning from sweet Dr. Jekyll into fierce Mr. Hyde, the exact opposite happens. ←

This is what <u>I</u> would sneak into Mr. Lambaste's coffee. (Hey, maybe into Cleo's hot chocolate too while I'm at it.)

That's another reason chemistry is more useful than biology. Besides not wanting to do dissections. I'm still hoping we can skip those and take apart something fun instead, like Mr. Potato Head.

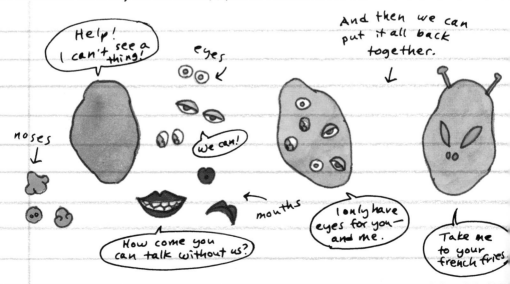

So science is good like I thought it would be, but I'm still not sure about art. I __want__ to like it because I love to draw. But everything is different in middle school. Maybe I'll start loving the stuff I used to hate (like math) and hating the stuff I used to love. I'm already beginning to hate English because of Mr. Lambaste, even though that was my favorite subject last year. It's bad when so much depends on __who__ does the teaching, not __what's__ being taught.

I mean, I love drawing the way _I_ want to draw. I'm not sure about Star's way.

Class, I know this looks like a bowl of fruit, but I don't want you to draw apples and lemons. I want you to draw the underlying shapes. Cezanne, a famous painter, said that all of nature can be reduced to basic shapes like the sphere, cylinder, and cone. I want you to SEE the shapes in the fruit and draw them. Okay?

not this↑

but this↗   ←yum—a delicious bowl of shapes!

It's funny—now I see shapes EVERY WHERE.

not a hand, but a circle with cylinders

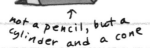
not a pencil, but a cylinder and a cone

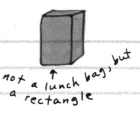
not a lunch bag, but a rectangle

Maybe I can simplify middle school by cutting it down into basic shapes. Hey, I just realized I'm doing a kind of dissection! Not like in science where you use a knife and there's blood, guts, and the gross smell of formaldehyde, but one where you use your eyes and brain. Like, take a tough-looking 8th grader.

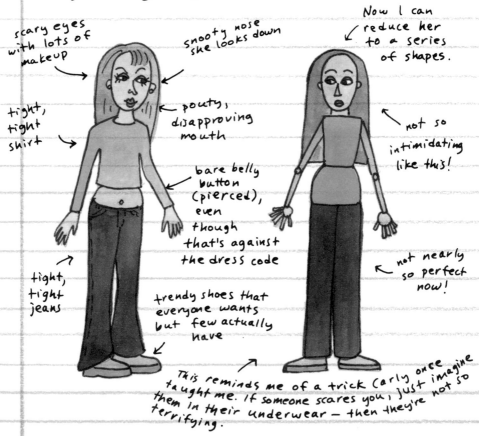

scary eyes with lots of makeup

snooty nose she looks down

Now I can reduce her to a series of shapes.

tight, tight shirt

pouty, disapproving mouth

not so intimidating like this!

bare belly button (pierced), even though that's against the dress code

tight, tight jeans

not nearly so perfect now!

trendy shoes that everyone wants but few actually have

This reminds me of a trick Carly once taught me. If someone scares you, just imagine them in their underwear — then they're not so terrifying.

Except for Mr. Lambaste. He's much scarier —and grosser—
if I imagine _him_ without clothes. YUCCH! It's better
to turn him into simple shapes instead.

Now he looks
like a tangram...

...or a robot.

shapes or
a bird?

shapes or an
ice cream cone?

The question is, what kind of shape am I in? Am I
strong enough to stand up to Mr. Lambaste? Am I tough
enough for middle school?

I thought Cleo and I had an agreement to stay as far away from each other as possible, but now that she knows I have Mr. Lambaste, she <u>wants</u> him to see us together.

I feel like I'm learning some simple addition:

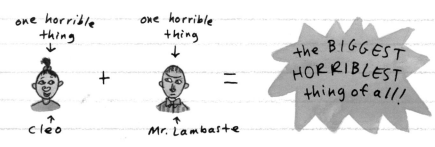

one horrible thing ↓ Cleo + one horrible thing ↓ Mr. Lambaste = the BIGGEST HORRIBLEST thing of all!

I knew having Cleo in the same school as me would be a disaster — I just didn't know how BIG a disaster it would be. It's not fair that I have to ward off <u>her</u> reputation. Why should <u>I</u> be judged by <u>her</u> behavior?

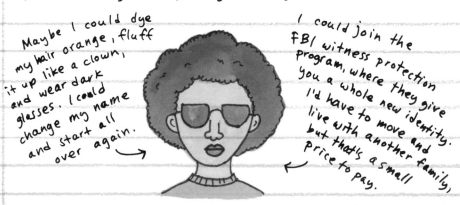

Maybe I could dye my hair orange, fluff it up like a clown, and wear dark glasses. I could change my name and start all over again. →

← I could join the FBI witness protection program, where they give you a whole new identity. I'd have to move and live with another family, but that's a small price to pay.

Saved by the bell!

Time for class!

At least Cleo can't follow me into class. →

In science I'm learning to see more clearly in a different way too. Not in cutting things open to see what's inside (PHEW!), but in seeing stuff that's too tiny to see with just your eyes. We're using the microscope to study what's inside of a puddle. It's amazing! With only your eyes you think there's dirt and water, maybe an old wad of gum or a bug or two, but nothing else.

what there really is
↓

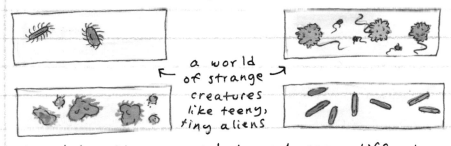

a world of strange creatures like teeny, tiny aliens

I wish I could use special glasses to see a different person entirely when I look at Cleo, like those 3-D glasses you use to look at special 3-D pictures. Not that I want Cleo to pop out of the background MORE. Just the opposite! I want her to blend right in, like camouflage glasses.

now you see her
↓

now you don't
↓

Yak, yak...

...yak!

and you don't hear her either!

That gave me an idea! Maybe Mr. L. just needs to see who I _really_ am instead of assuming I'm like Cleo. How can I show him the real Amelia?

The problem is, you can't tell the real you by your face. So how do I make myself different from Cleo? I mean MORE different than I already am.
↓

Mirror, mirror, on the wall, how can I look _least_ Cleo of all?

I asked Carly what she would do. How can I make myself as UN-Cleo as possible? Or if I can't help but look like Cleo's sister, maybe I could make myself invisible, like dye my hair pink and wear all-pink clothes so you can't tell me apart from the Pepto-Bismol pink walls in the classrooms.

Carly didn't think I should change my looks at all. "That's not how you'll get him to see the real you," she said. Instead she had a completely different idea.

Another great thing about Carly is she never panics. She's calm in the <u>worst</u> situations.

Why don't you do something nice for Mr. Lambaste to prove to him that you don't play mean tricks like Cleo? You could bake him some cookies or fudge.

That's a terrific idea! Carly even promised to come to my house after school and help me bake our favorite cookies.

CHOCOLATE-CHIP PEPPERMINT COOKIES

3/4 c. butter
1 egg
1 tsp. vanilla
1/4 tsp. salt
1 c. chocolate chips

1/2 c. brown sugar
1/2 c. granulated sugar
1 tsp. peppermint extract
1 tsp. baking soda
1 1/2 c. flour

Cream butter and sugars together. Add eggs, vanilla, and peppermint. Add flour, salt, and baking soda. Mix well with chocolate chips. Bake 12-15 minutes at 350°

(leo, the pig, ate way more than her share, but I saved enough cookies to make a nice present for Mr. L.

I wrapped the plate of cookies with a pretty ribbon so it would look extra special. And I put a nice card on it so that if I lose my nerve at the last minute and just leave it on his desk, he'll still know it's from me.

No one can say this isn't a <u>sweet</u> present!

Here's what I thought would happen:

This is what really happened:

Now I have detention! I've NEVER gotten detention in my LIFE! And now I get it for doing something nice?! IT'S NOT FAIR!

I almost cried, but there was NO WAY I was going to let that mean ogre think he had any power over my feelings. It was the longest morning ever. I just stared at the table, biting my lip, working on NOT crying.

I sat frozen at lunchtime. →

I wasn't hungry at all. ↙

↑

And I didn't care what table I sat at. I could have been in the janitor's closet for all I cared.

Carly came up to me. "Well, how did it go?" she asked. "Solved your problem with Mr. L., didn't I?"

I couldn't open my mouth. The words felt like heavy rocks sunk to the bottom of my stomach. I couldn't get them to rise to my lips.

"Amelia, how did it go? Amelia? Um, did something happen?"

All the tears I'd been holding in for so long just burst out. I was embarrassed about crying, but Carly's a good friend. She put her arm around me and waited for me to calm down.

There's NOTHING I can do! He'll ALWAYS assume the worst of me!

And now I have DETENTION!!

That's terrible!

He's such a jerk!

Carly thought I should complain to the principal, but I'm afraid that if I do, I'll just get another detention. Maybe the best idea is to pretend to be invisible this year. After a while Mr. L. might even forget I'm in his class. I wish I could forget I'm there.

I could wear a bag over my head so he couldn't tell it was me. →

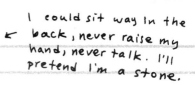

← I could sit way in the back, never raise my hand, never talk. I'll pretend I'm a stone.

It was hard to concentrate in my other classes until I got to art and Star let us use pastels. Real art supplies! Normally that would put me in a great mood, but all I could think about was what was coming <u>after</u> school, not what we were doing during school.

← cool pastels in cool colors →

And for once Star gave us a fun assignment. We were supposed to draw something —anything — but we couldn't use the real colors. She showed us some famous paintings with blue horses and green faces as examples.

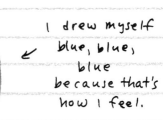

← I drew myself blue, blue, blue because that's how I feel.

Picasso had a famous period of painting called his "blue period" when everything he painted had lots of blue in it. He did a lot of sad-looking clowns and musicians. Everyone was not only blue, they looked gaunt and miserable. That's how I feel — scooped out and empty.

And then I had detention and felt even bluer. I went from pale, washed-out gray blue to deep, dark Prussian blue.

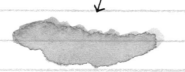 

So, now I know what detention is like:

Boring

Embarrassing

Boring

Humiliating

Boring

And more boring

Mr. L. came into the room to check on us. There were eleven kids, me, Carly, two boys I know, Max and Omar, and some kids I don't know.

And you, young lady, why are you here? This isn't study hall.

I'm keeping Amelia company.

How noble of you. Too bad it's not allowed. This isn't a friendship club. Now leave before I assign detention to you for real—tomorrow.

Almost as bad as being in detention is being lumped with the other kids who are being punished. I mean, I didn't throw paper airplanes or break the skeleton in science class. I wasn't loud, rude, or disruptive. My crime was baking cookies. Some crime.

The other kids didn't seem at all embarrassed about being in detention. They must be used to it, like it's just a regular part of the school day. Whenever Mr. L. wasn't looking, some kids shot spitballs at the ceiling. They told me they were trying to recreate the Big Dipper and Orion, making constellations out of wadded, chewed-up paper.

It's not exactly the ceiling of the Sistine Chapel, but watching them aim, shoot, and high-five whenever a good one stuck made it a lot less boring.

Kids in Detention Land

asleep kids, drooling on the desk
↓

scary, goth kids
↓

black, black eyes
↘

We'll all be swallowed up by the eternal Ring of Fire.

black lipstick
←

Death to the universe.

← antsy kids, jiggling legs up and down and driving everyone crazy

↑
crackling with nervous energy

It's so...

I know...

Cool kids — even in detention, there's something about them that makes them untouchably cool.
↓

Let's go...

↑ leaning back in chairs until mr. L. yells at them to stop it

Carly called me after dinner. "You're right," she said. "He's impossible. Maybe your idea to pretend you're invisible is the best strategy after all." That didn't exactly make me feel better.

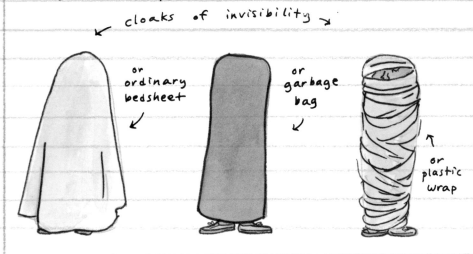

cloaks of invisibility

or ordinary bedsheet

or garbage bag

or plastic wrap

Today I tried Plan B. I called it Stonehenge because the plan was to sit frozen like a stone so Mr. L. wouldn't notice me and would leave me alone. I thought it would be hard to stay so still, but it wasn't since I felt like a big, sad lump. A bigger, sadder lump after a morning with Mr. L. — Plan B was a complete failure! It didn't matter that I didn't DO anything — Mr. L. was still horrible to me. He didn't give me detention, but he made nasty cracks about me in front of the whole class. Then I really wished I was invisible.

Open your books to page 36. We're going to read a poem where the writer describes the beauty and grace of a swan.

Why don't you start, Amelia, if it isn't too difficult for you to say the word "grace," considering you have so little of it yourself.

Now we're going to work on our maps of the Roman Empire. Make sure you label everything neatly. We can't all be slobs like Amelia here.

I just kept telling myself, I'm NOT a slob and I DO have grace (I think). But why would a teacher be so mean? I could barely read the poem, my voice wobbled so much. For that I really needed to pretend I was made of stone. By lunchtime my stomach hurt so much from Mr. L.'s comments that I couldn't eat anything. Carly tried to make me feel better, but NOTHING could make me feel better — except an asteroid falling on Mr. L. or an alien abducting him.

Mom used to always say, "Sticks and stones may break your bones, but words will never hurt you." She's WRONG — words can be vicious and sharp and more cutting than any knife!

↓

← These are painless in comparison!

Then a light went on! Being nice didn't work. Being invisible didn't work.

IDEA

I should be mean! If Mr. L's going to punish me no matter what I do, I might as well enjoy myself and really do something wrong.

I felt like I was in one of those cartoons with a devil whispering on one shoulder and an angel on the other.

Let's think of something REALLY nasty. He deserves it!

Just because he's mean doesn't mean you should be too.

He's going to punish you anyway. Why not earn it?

Do you want to be like Cleo? Do you want him to be right?

That's it! No matter what, I DON'T want to be ANYTHING like Cleo! But there's got to be something I can do besides being insulted all morning. I've got to get a real idea.

Good thing art class is turning out so much better.
I was worried at first, but now I like trying new things. This
week we're working on linoleum block prints. It's tricky because
you have to think backward. What you carve will end up the
white of the paper, and what you _don't_ carve gets ink on it
and ends up black. Instead of drawing lines, you take away
everything EXCEPT the lines you want left. I guess it's kind
of like sculpture, only two-dimensional.

For example,
this block...
↓

...prints like
this.
↓

I wish I could
see Mr. L.
in reverse.
↳

I'd love to turn his
dark parts into light ones ↑

   It's funny — art, science, Cleo, Mr. Lambarte — they're
all making me look at myself and the world differently.
From breaking complicated shapes into simple ones, looking
beyond what you can see with your naked eye, and now seeing
things in negative space rather than positive space. It's like
everything is combining to tell me that things _aren't_ what
they appear to be. You have to look closer to really understand them.
   Wait a minute, does that mean I have to study Cleo?

Is there more to _her_ than meets the eye? YUCCCH! And Mr. Lambaste? I sure don't want to understand him — that's waaaay too close for comfort. Maybe sometimes it's better NOT to see well. It might be nice to need glasses because when you take them off, the world becomes a nice, big blur. There's something safe and cozy about that.

It's like the cartoon of the old lady and the monster.
As long as she can't see him clearly, she's not afraid of him.

It's funny that art, the class that's considered the least serious and important — after all, it's an elective, so you don't have to take it, and there's no homework — is teaching me the most stuff, things I can use in the rest of my life, not just in art class.

And Star is nice to me. She doesn't think I'm a clumsy slob.

Good work, Amelia. I love how you're using the darks and lights to shade — very good.

It's a good thing that art and science, my two favorite subjects, are the last classes of the day (depending, of course, on what day it is and whether it's an A week or a B week). When they're last, I don't have to go home with the bad taste of Mr. L. in my mouth (though it's no treat facing him first thing in the morning either). And I need some teacher to like me. Or at least not hate me.

On the walk home from school all the houses looked so cozy and warm, like perfect, happy people lived there, living perfect, happy lives. I know that's not true, that lots of people have problems, like world hunger and global warming and child labor and bad TV reception. But lately I feel like I'm the only miserable kid on the planet. It may not be true (I know it's not true), but that's how it feels.

Luckily, just when I really needed something to cheer me up, I got it. A postcard from Nadia was waiting for me on the kitchen table!

Dear Amelia,
~~Sorry~~ to hear about the mean teacher. That's ~~so~~ unfair to be judged by ~~Cleo's~~ reputation! (I'm ~~so~~ glad I'm an only child!) If I were you, I'd write a letter to the teacher explaining exactly how you feel. Or write a story about it. A story is a good way to get your point across without seeming like you're accusing him.
~~Good luck!~~
    Yours till the stamp pads, Nadia

PERK-O-LATER

23¢

Amelia
564 North Homerest
Oopa, Oregon
97881

It was almost as good as having her over to my house. I could hear her voice and see her smile. Nadia's the kind of friend that no matter how far away she is or how little we get to see each other, I still feel close to her.

And I love her idea! I'm not sure about a letter, but I can try writing a story.

Not a Story Book but a Book Story

There was a boy who really loved to read. Every week he would go to the library, bring home a pile of books, and spend the rest of the day reading.

It's too exciting to stop now!

One day he went to the library as usual, but it was closed for painting. Disappointed, the boy went home, desperate to find a book to read. He looked all over his house for something he hadn't already read, but the only book he could find had a cheesy cover with big, raised letters practically yelling the title at you.

It looked so stupid, the boy barely wanted to touch it, much less read it.

But it was that book or nothing. Holding his nose, the boy opened to the first page. After the first sentence he couldn't stop reading! It was more than a good book—it was GREAT, the kind of book you remember for the rest of your life!

What he needed was superhero x-ray vision so he could see beyond the distracting, sleazy cover to the true nature of the book.

Moral of the story: You can't tell what something — or someone — is like just by looking. You have to get to know them. Wait a second, isn't there a saying about this? Oh, yeah — you can't judge a book by its cover. Well, you can't judge a person by their cover either.

It's not a bad story, but it's not very original. I made a copy of it and put it in an envelope with Mr. L.'s name on it. I could leave it on his desk when he's not looking. And keep my fingers crossed that he gets the hint. Only it's not a very subtle hint. Maybe it will make him hate me even more.

Wait, I have a better idea for a different story. One that's not so obvious, one that doesn't sound like a cliché grown-ups are always telling you (like "waste not, want not," "early to bed, early to rise, makes a man healthy, wealthy, and wise," "an apple a day keeps the doctor away," or "to give is better than to receive").

I'm not sure I believe those sayings anyway, especially the one about giving. I love getting presents way more than giving them — there's NO comparison. Unless the saying is about giving germs, not gifts — then I agree entirely.

Cleo giving the gift that goes on giving →

Ah-choo!

The Girl with the Magic Eyes

Once there was a girl with an amazing magical ability. She could look at anything and see it for what it really was. Sometimes that was bad (or a little annoying), like there was no way to surprise her with a present because she knew what it was without even unwrapping it.

Most of the time, though, it was a very handy trick. She could glance at a bathroom door and know if it was gross inside or if it was clean and had toilet paper.

The best part was the way she could see deep into people, into what they were really like. It was incredible how wrong you could be about someone if you judged them just by how they looked.

The girl could see:

that the tough-looking 8th grader who always looked like she was ready to bite your head off...→

...was really a sweet older sister who took good care of her baby brother.

that the mean old man who waved his cane at you and yelled to leave the pigeons alone...

...was really lonely and missed his children and grandchildren desperately.

that the boy who sat at the back of the class and never raised his hand or said anything interesting...

...was really full of ideas for cool inventions and fantastic stories, and if you listened to him, he wasn't boring at all like you thought he was.

But sometimes the inside and the outside of a person matched perfectly and the girl could see that, too.

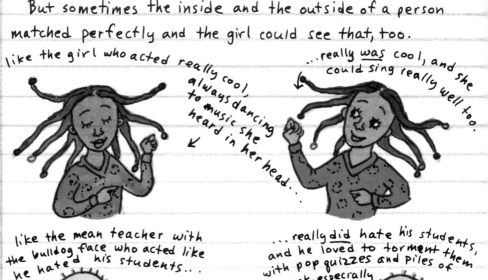

like the girl who acted really cool, always dancing to music she heard in her head...

...really _was_ cool, and she could sing really well too.

like the mean teacher with the bulldog face who acted like he hated his students...

...really did hate his students, and he loved to torment them with pop quizzes and piles of homework, especially right before and after vacations.

If you think I have this job because I like kids and I like teaching them — THINK AGAIN!

Hee, hee, hee. Let's see how they like a 20-page report — due TOMORROW!

Then one day the girl met a boy she couldn't read at all. The harder she looked at him, the less clear her sense of him was. When she looked at anyone else, it was like seeing through a window, but with him it was like peering into a fog that gets thicker and thicker the more you stare at it.

The boy was a complete blank to her.

She wondered what he could be inside. And what it would be like to get to know someone slowly, not all at once.

She was curious what it would be like to get to know him the old-fashioned way, by talking with him and noticing what he liked and didn't like. Instead of seeing him all at once, she learned to understand him bit by bit. It wasn't easy at all. It was hard work getting to know a person that way. But it was also exciting and interesting. And the boy became her friend the way no one else ever had.

And the girl liked that her friend wasn't easy for her to read. She liked him all the more because she had to be patient and every new thing she learned about him was like getting a little present, a surprise she couldn't guess about. And with time she found it wasn't hard work after all — it was just a matter of opening her eyes wider and waiting to see the rainbow through the fog.

The End

Now <u>that's</u> a better story. I wish I had magical eyes like that girl. Maybe I do. Maybe that's what art is teaching me — how to see more clearly. And maybe if I give <u>this</u> story to Mr. L. instead of the other one, he'll see <u>me</u> more clearly. It's worth trying.

I felt lucky about my story (something I haven't felt for a long time). Lucky enough to dare to slip it in an envelope onto Mr. L.'s desk. Except I wasn't lucky after all. Mr. L. saw me. But he didn't see what I was doing and, of course, he assumed the worst.

WHAT do you think you're doing? Are you trying to steal tomorrow's quiz from my desk so you can cheat? First you try to poison me— DON'T deny it. I know what you're up to. And now you're a cheater. I knew you were trouble the second I saw you. Trouble!

Did you think detention was bad before? How would you like a MONTH of it?

I couldn't answer. My tongue was frozen cold in my mouth. A cheater?! ← Me?!

I knew what was bad — and it wasn't detention, it wasn't me, it was HIM! I thought writing the story helped me feel better, but that was erased by Mr. L's savage voice, by his UNFAIR accusation. I couldn't take it anymore.

Actually I was very, very calm, but the block of ice that was my tongue melted, and suddenly I couldn't stop talking. Maybe the story gave me some kind of power.

I am NOT a cheater! I've NEVER cheated!

And I didn't try to poison you! I was being nice!

I baked you cookies. GOOD, SWEET, DELICIOUS cookies!

"Are you finished?" was all Mr. L. said in his steely, cold voice. I nodded. "Then sit down and be quiet."

I was so angry and afraid at the same time I was shaking. I tried to calm myself down by taking deep, slow breaths. I couldn't concentrate on anything in class, but at least I felt better — the way you feel better after you throw up when you have stomach flu. And I made a decision. I'm NOT letting Mr. L. insult me anymore. If he makes a nasty crack, I'm answering him back. Just knowing that made me feel stronger inside. I felt like I was finally seeing something for what it was, both in Mr. L. and in myself. I didn't have to believe his version of me, and I didn't have to care what he thought. That was _his_ problem, not mine.

When the bell finally rang and it was time for lunch, I felt like I'd been asleep — or frozen— for a million years. My legs were stiff and wooden, and my fingers felt thick and clumsy gathering up my stuff. I had this horrible dread that Mr. L. was going to grab me when I walked past his desk to the door, like he would grow a tentacle that would whip out and choke me, but I didn't dare look at him. I stared straight ahead and held my breath until I was safely in the hall.

In the normal light of the cafeteria I felt much better, like I'd been let out of prison and could gulp in fresh air again. I looked around and saw where Carly was sitting with some other kids. That was the table where I belonged. Suddenly I was starving.

A cheese and cucumber sandwich had never tasted so good.

No apple was as crisply perfect as this one!

At lunch I told Carly everything. I can't change Mr. L., but I can change how I think of him. If I don't care about his opinion, his insults can't hurt me.

I'm so proud of you, Amelia — you really stood up for yourself!

I am too. It was scary, but now that it's over, I feel so much better! I just need to remember, Mr. L. is a JERK!

The funny thing was, the rest of my day wasn't ruined like I thought it would be. In math, fractions, which have never behaved well for me, stopped acting up and did what they were supposed to do.

And in science I drew pictures of the crystals we studied under the microscope. They were amazing — teeny, tiny, incredibly beautiful worlds.

But the best part was art. I didn't have to struggle to make myself see the negative space in my linoleum print. I could tell exactly where I needed to cut and what I needed to leave behind. It was like a light had turned on in my brain. I even finished the block. It looks great! I'm not sure which I like better, the block or the printed image.

block

print

Somehow, even though it was such an awful morning, I felt lighter than I had since school started. Even my backpack couldn't weigh me down.

What are you so happy about?

Nothing you'd understand.

← Even Cleo seemed nicer.

Seeing Cleo on the way home normally would bug me, but not today. I wonder how long this will last, this feeling of being so completely myself, nothing can touch me. That's what it is — I don't feel like I'm Cleo's sister, or Mr. L.'s pet grudge, or a nobody who doesn't have a place to sit in the cafeteria.

I stared at the stars for a long time before going to bed, wanting to hold on to that feeling for as long as I could. I thought of having detention and Max and Omar's spitball constellations. I couldn't help smiling.

I thought I would be scared going to school today, that the strong feeling from yesterday would disappear. But it didn't. I felt fine walking into Mr. L.'s class. Then I saw something on my desk.

It was the story I'd written. And at the bottom there was a tiny red "A" and the comment "Good work. I consider this → extra credit."

How did Mr. L. know this was _my_ story? And did that mean he didn't hate me anymore? Or if he did still hate me, as long as I get good grades, does it matter?

I didn't have a chance to think about what it all meant and whether I should be scared or worried or what. Before I could sort it all out, Mr. L. walked in the door. He looked the same, he acted the same, but something seemed different about him. I stared at him hard. I wasn't going to look away. His face wasn't any softer, and he still glared at me when he passed by (at least, I think it was a glare — or maybe it's his unibrow that makes him look like he's perpetually scowling). But he wasn't so scary somehow. Maybe it's not him that's changed — it's me. I should be more terrified of him than ever, but I'm not. I don't know why, I just am not.

I know I look the same old way, but I don't <u>feel</u> the same old way.

I'm stronger and tougher, like I passed a hard physical challenge—scaled a tall, tall wall or climbed a high, high mountain.

Or maybe it's just that I'm in middle school. Maybe I'm a little bit closer to being a 16-year-old than a 6-year-old after all.

THE REAL USEFUL

Table of Teachers

Teachers to be avoided at all costs:

Miss Troy — WAY too much homework.

Mrs. Kittredge — she'd be okay if she would just shave off her beard. It's hard to concentrate when you're trying desperately NOT to look at her chin.

Mr. Lambaste — HORRIBLE IN EVERY WAY — has favorites and favorite enemies, is mean, vicious, and unfair!

Teachers to try to get:

Ms. Demille — every other Friday shows movies and brings in popcorn — SWEET!

Mr. Hiyashi — plays cool music when he's in a good mood.

Mr. Lubov — everyone loves him and says he's the best even though you have to work hard.

Mrs. Wold — has traveled all over the world and has great stories to tell.

INFORMATION

Table of Toilets

Bathrooms NEVER to use:

The one on the 2nd floor near Mrs. Kittredge's class.

The one by the front office.

The one in the library.

You want smelly and disgusting?

Just visit me!

Dining Table

Translation of Cafeteria Menu:

Chicken Caesar Salad — 3 pieces of dry, stringy chicken, wilted lettuce, and rubbery croutons. (Doesn't that negate the whole idea of croutons — they're there to be crunchy!) DO NOT EAT!

Taco Salad — Crumbled beef that tastes like clumpy sand, soggy lettuce, tomatoes that are so unripe they're like chewing on grass, salsa that still tastes like the tin can it came in, and four tortilla chips (no more, no less, always exactly four). You can eat the chips, but forget about the rest!

This notebook is dedicated to
Paula,
with gratitude for letting Amelia finally
graduate from elementary school,
and to
Elias, Mia, and Emma,
for enduring middle school and living
to tell the tale.